FREE

SANDOL STODDARD

Illustrated by Jenni Oliver

Houghton Mifflin Company Boston
1976

For Zoila

Library of Congress Cataloging in Publication Data

Warburg, Sandol Stoddard.
 Free.

 SUMMARY: A fable in which a courageous young girl
and her companions are freed by the sacrifice of a perfect rose.
 [1. Fables] I. Oliver, Jenni. II. Title.
PZ8.2.W28Fr   398.2   75-40013
ISBN 0-395-24210-X

Once in the land of Sharon far away there was a castle
in a wood; and in the middle of the castle there was a garden where children played. At the very center of the
garden was a rose growing all alone. It was a red, red rose,
far more beautiful than any rose the children had ever
seen; but that may have been because in all the world at
that time, it was the only one.

From the wild wood around the castle came hungry tigers trying to get in. Luckily, there were unicorns in the garden who fought fiercely every night at the gates, so that for a long time the children were quite safe. During all the years when the children were very young, the tigers came only after dark.

And so time went on. By day the unicorns lay beneath the trees and slept, and the children played hide-and-seek in the corners of the garden. The rose stood up on its stem at the center of everything, with its green leaves all around it, always perfect and always the same. Sometimes the children looked at it and wondered about it, and sometimes they did not; but always and always they knew that it was there.

After a number of years the children began to notice something rather curious. The more they grew up, the more, in some mysterious fashion, the unicorns grew down. That is to say, as the children grew larger, the unicorns, who were their champions and protectors, grew smaller and smaller. It was alarming. The children worried about it a great deal, for it seemed to them that one day sooner or later their battle must be lost. They could not help growing up, and yet, they did not know how to fight tigers themselves. There seemed to be nothing to do about it but wait and hope.

At last the King of the Tigers came striding in bright daylight straight up to the castle gate and shouted, "Hallo there! The time has come for us to make a bargain. All we want is that one, insignificant little red rose, you know. Only give it to us and we will go away and never bother you again. But hurry up about it, or you will be sorry."

The children shivered and looked at one another. Then their leader, who was a boy called Pert, spoke up and said loudly, "Stay away from us tonight, O King, and we will give the rose to you in the morning, I promise."

Now, Pert's real name was Expert, because he was so good at fooling everybody. He was very, very tricky and clever, which in fact was why the children had chosen him for their leader when they were very young. This time he meant to show them what he could do in a truly great emergency. Grinning to himself and rubbing his hands together, Pert made his way to his own secret hiding place in the garden and went to work. He was going to trick the tigers now, once and for all.

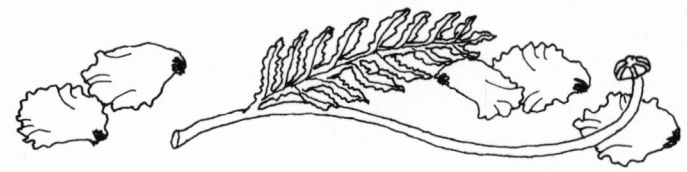

The tigers prowled around the castle walls throughout the night. Meantime, Pert gathered up the petals of red poppies and tied them very, very carefully together with blades of grass so that they looked — well, almost exactly like a rose.

In the morning he walked briskly out the gate and handed the false rose to the Tiger King. "Here you are," he said. "This is what you wanted. We have kept our promise, so now you must go away and leave us in peace, as you promised!"

But the King of the Tigers simply laughed. Oh, how he laughed! Then he opened his mouth very wide and gobbled up Pert in one gulp; so that was the end of him. The Tiger King went off into the forest still laughing, with the make-believe rose tucked behind his ear.

Soon the King of the Tigers came back again. The leader of the children now was a strict and proper girl named Prim. "Oh pretty one," the King purred to her in a silky, flattering manner, "only give us that one red rose, for pity's sake." Then he rolled on the ground as if he had a terrible stomach ache. "Oh, oh, oh," he groaned pathetically. "We tigers are suffering so, and nothing will cure us of our pains but the rose from your garden. Bring it here to me, I beg you, sweet lady, and then I promise that we will go far away from you forever."

Prim patted him nicely on the head and replied, "I will have to see about the rules before I do that, you know. We have a great many rules and regulations in our garden now, and it is up to me to see that everything is done properly." Then she smiled sweetly at the Tiger King and called him "Sire" and "Your Majesty" several times, and asked him politely if he would come back in the morning. The Tiger King went away grumbling to the forest.

This left Prim with a rather alarming problem. She had been chosen as leader because of all the helpful rules she made; and yet she suddenly realized that not a single one of them had anything to do with the rose. The rose was just *there*, as it had been from the beginning; and Prim herself had never stopped to think very much about it.

She and the other children sat down together to talk things over. They knew that there was only one rose in the world and that they themselves could never make another. They could not imagine their lives without the castle, and they could not imagine the castle without the garden, or the garden without the rose. Surely the rose could not be given away; but what were they to do when the Tiger King came back in the morning?

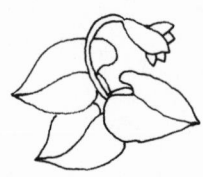

"I don't believe he meant a word of it," said Prim. "I think he is just trying to trick us and fool us and scare us away. I don't even believe he is a King." And when morning came, she marched out the castle gate with her nose in the air, prepared to tell that tiger a thing or two.

The Tiger King came bounding up to her and sniffed all around her hands to see what she had brought for him. "No, I didn't bring you the rose," said Prim. "You are just a silly animal trying to pretend that you are important, and I am not afraid of you one bit. So *there*!" She turned on her heel and began to walk away from him. But the Tiger King laughed and laughed, and he followed her. Then he opened his huge jaws and gobbled her up too; and that was the end of Prim.

The gate was open. With his tail switching back and forth the Tiger King marched straight into the middle of the garden. In a twinkling the unicorns vanished deep into the ferns. The children hid themselves away in the darker thickets as he approached. For a long moment the Tiger King stood in front of the little rosebush, staring at the one great blossom there. He ground his teeth together and his jaws began to drool with anticipation. He walked around the rosebush snarling cheerfully, just to let everyone know who was in charge of the situation, and he butted at it several times with his head. A few of the petals fell down, but the rose went on blooming.

Then the King of the Tigers made a running leap. He gobbled down the red rose in one huge gulp. He swallowed hard and licked his lips, and then he turned and began to prance proudly out of the garden.

At that moment a new sound came into the world for the first time. It was the sound of children crying quietly, not even wondering whether anyone hears them or not. It was different from the crying of a person who is calling for help. It was the sort of crying that sounds as if it will go on forever, because there is no hope.

The Tiger King heard it and he was pleased. He thought it was the most delightful sound he had ever heard in all his life. He lifted up his head to laugh out loud again; but then he suddenly realized that something strange was happening to him. Something was stuck down in his throat. It was a thorn from the stem of the rose.

The Tiger King coughed a little and tried to swallow the thorn. Then he roared furiously and tried to cough it up, but that did not help either. In a few more moments the Tiger King lay on the ground, choking and gasping and clawing at the earth with all his might. The children stopped crying and watched him, because it was such a strange sight to see. They wondered what would happen next.

"Do you think he will say now that he is sorry?" asked one small boy.

"No," replied another boy. "He won't say anything at all, ever again. He can't."

"I wonder if he *is* sorry," said the smallest girl, who was still too young to have a name all of her own. Suddenly she knew that she must find out the truth. "Watch out," cried the other children, but the smallest girl walked straight up to the dying tiger and looked deep into his eyes. What she saw there made her shiver. "He is not sorry at all," she told the others. "He is lying here wishing that he could get well and eat up all the rest of us."

So the King of the Tigers put down his head and died; and that was the end of him. The children dug him a grave and buried him at the foot of the ruined rosebush, with its broken, empty stem. From that day the other tigers went far away, and although their growling and snarling could sometimes be heard from a distance, they were seldom seen in that part of the world again.

Everything was changed now, for better or for worse. The land of Sharon was at peace, and so the gates of the castle were left wide open. Deer, rabbits and foxes darted in and out; green moss grew over the rusty locks

and hinges of the gates. The smallest girl could now lift the largest of the unicorns up into her arms. Thus they stood together often, looking long and long into the darkness of the forest beyond. Gradually the unicorns ventured out, growing smaller yet. Some of them grew wings and flew away; others made their nests in heaps of dry leaves under the great oak trees. There they lived on milkweed and cobwebs, coming out to play only by the light of the moon, so that after a time, most of the children forgot to notice them any more.

The children by now had decided to make their home in the forest. The castle and the garden were not the same any more. The magic — or so they thought — was gone. The children grew older yet, and learned to gather wild berries and watercress; and they made houses

for themselves in the treetops or by the banks of running streams. It was a good life, although there were many things the children were careful not to think about, even in their dreams.

It was the smallest girl who still thought very quietly to herself about all that had happened so long ago. Many and many a time she dreamed of the garden, and of the rose. When she wakened in the morning it was hard for her sometimes to believe that she was now in such a differ-ent place. At moments like these a great sadness would come over her; but she kept this sadness deep in her heart, and let no one see it, and spoke of it to no one.

Meantime, she who had been so small had grown tall and marvelously strong. She had built a fine hut for herself in the forest, and had planted vegetables and fruits enough for herself and all her friends to eat. Because she always sang and danced at her work, her friends had given her the name of Free. There were no leaders in the group now, for none were needed. But Free was so generous, and so full of zest and of sweetness and of joy, that she had become everyone's favorite. Day by day the others came to her for the sharing of all the things that can be spoken, even without words.

One day Free knew that she must go on a journey, and that she must go alone. She could wait no longer. She must go back to the castle and back to the garden again. For years now, none of the children had even been willing to approach the gates. They tried to tell themselves that this was because they did not care any more about the garden or about the rose. They told one another that their old home was not worth remembering in any case — that nothing from the past was worth remembering. The truth was that their sadness and their disappointment had made them afraid. But Free was not afraid.

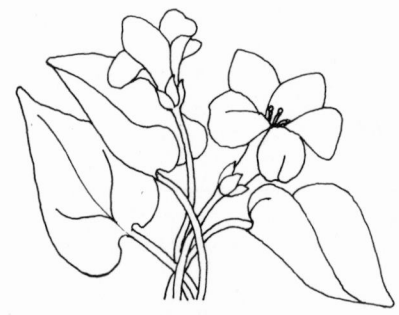

I am not afraid, she said to herself as she made her way barefoot over the path through the forest. At least, I am not *very* much afraid. The important thing for Free was to go and look once more at the garden for herself, just as she had gone to see the truth in the eyes of the dying tiger. If it had become an ugly place, a place only of sadness and bad memories, then it would be better for her to know it. The broken stem of the rosebush must be looked at. The mound in the earth where the tiger's body had lain must be looked at, and seen. She would do it, and then — then she did not know what would happen.

The walls were all grown over with vines; she could hardly find the gate. Her heart pounded and she trembled as at last she made her way, stumbling, through the entrance and into the great, green space within. The castle walls cast a golden light over everything. How vast it

all was! How many pathways and passageways she found,
searching for the center of the garden! Singing birds were
all around her, rustling and calling in the enormous ferns.

Finally her foot struck a soft place in the earth beneath
her, and she fell. Rising to her feet, she realized that she
had come at last to the place. The tiger's grave was cov-
ered over with a deep, bright carpet of flowering moss, and
it was here that she had tumbled down.

The rose was gone, of course — and yet, when she
looked up again into the space above the mound, Free
found that something else was there. Up and up and up

she looked. Where once had been a rosebush no taller than herself, there was now a mighty tree of splendid proportions. From the broken place in the stem that the tiger had destroyed had come springing branch after branch of new growth, soaring high into the sunlit air like a fountain of green water spangled with leaves. From each sturdy branch grew a multitude of stems; and at the end of each stem there bloomed a great, red rose.

The air was perfumed all around her with their scent. Free reached out her arms and cried aloud with joy. At her cry, a flock of butterflies lifted their wings and fluttered from the flowering moss at her feet toward the sky, brushing gently against her face and against the palms of her hands. There were hundreds of roses now — thousands, perhaps. There were roses to look at, roses to touch, to smell — roses to pluck and transplant in every glade and dell of the forest. There were roses enough to transform the forest itself into a garden such as the world had never known.

But, oh, first, she thought — first of all, this wonder and this glory must be shared. She turned to cry out to the others, to call to them and tell every one of her friends what she had found. Yet already they had missed their favorite; even now they were searching for her and following her. She could hear their running footsteps coming closer now, and in another moment their glad voices rang out all around her in the garden, calling her name.